I0739967

SAUDADE

SAUDADE

Written by
NIHAL BHAGWANDAS

Saudade

ISBN: 978-0-9924486-0-8

Cover Creation and Formatting   :   Sal Doud at UniverSal Designs
                                    Salimdaoud7@gmail.com
Front Cover Image   :   'Stain#1' by Justin Martino
                                    justinmartino@live.com.au
Manuscript Design   :   Richard Warneke at RW Marketing
                                    info@rwmarketing.com.au

A big thank you to my family and friends
for their constant support and belief and to Nicole,
who turned my world into something that was
just as real and as beautiful as my dreams.

'down the steps of my dreams and my weariness,
descend from your unreality, descend and be my substitute
for the world'

Fernando Pessoa.

In the melting formless hours that invade my consciousness I indulge in thoughtless aspiring memories of you and I. As vivid as the wine that intoxicates my being I travel through sonnets of desires that continuously play the medley of our passion. There has never been a higher plain to conquer than our lust. Infernos and volcanoes of fierce want that pours all over my body like water. A want so deep and strong that stars are born and die next to the burning of our bodies that seem to pale everything in comparison. In every waking walking thinking second of my days I spend awake I tear my mind to shreds with the one and only objection that is to lose myself in you again and again until I can not breathe without inhaling your scent in every moment of this personified time. And in my dreams I am plagued by the intimacy in which we languish and in every world that I travel to in my subconscious every gust of wind, every mountain that permeates and whispers into my bleeding ears, is your name which over powers every other emotion I have ever felt and torches them in a fire that lights up the entire universe and bands the heavens with traces of you and I for the rest of time.

Chasing shadows in images. The spirits follow. I revealed myself under the pale twilight eyes of the night. My pondering wallowing senses catch fire. Then burn out. This soul and this body, the trapping of life. Days lay out like flickering movies in black and white. Consciousness and bated breathes accumulate into echoes of shadows of existence, material worlds collide and these memories all have meanings. The path leads into avenues that I never pondered and in the burning alleyways of your desire, I lit small fires to keep the darkness from swallowing me whole. The situations of life, the moments we find ourselves in, if it weren't for the minutes before we would not be in this disposition. I fought and woke and everytime my eyes opened I salvaged a remnant of my dreams to hold on to and reflect on when I needed them. Memories got lost and buried underneath my eyes with crystal clarity. Hesitations and confounded conflicts. If only we could just be. And not worry about the ramifications. I sat on beaches and watched the sky unfold in turbulent angles of light. Seeing angels and heroes glistening in the lights of happier days. This world passes like peasant hands stealing in the early hours of yesterday. Songs and music, words and languished voices. There must be some kind of distant order, a shade of blue that the world has yet to see. Of all the labels that describe this life. How much more is there left to remain nameless? Some times moments, emotions, feelings they do not have one defining name, yet they do exist. We use objects and make sense of our surroundings but do we ever really know anything? We fade to dust. All these eyes and faces. There is always more. Always the unknown that will one day be known, maybe tomorrow or something, somewhere in a whisper, a scent or never at all.

In the fraction of an instant. You parade before my vision. Sights with no sounds, sounds that subliminally reproach the night. Your lips taste like a frenzied fevered wraith. Obsolete rainbows that no one ever really says they saw. There are worlds that exist in this one. Other eyes and novices that we are not trained to see. And in our waking hours we ponder our fantasies. Just as lonely and fevered as the ones before. Never after that relief do we ever ask for anything more. The truth hidden behind layers and layers of untruths. Sanctioned and medieval. We were never meant to hurt each other. Until we rest in peace. All our souls, entwined together. We'll never really know the light from the dark, the answers lie for us to ponder. But it will only make sense when we fade to dust. So silently and bitterly we walk through alleyways and corners of the unknown, only to never really know.

Neon nights. Heads gleam in bitter sweet moments of ecstasy. Each second more heightened then the last. More electric and sympathetic then yesterday, through neo classical light and reflections of omnipresent ghosts. We border on the brink of water coloured rainbows. In the edges of last years words and empty desires that I lay hinging on the brink of reality, I ponder these words and ways that will never be.

Scorned hearts. Fevered Pentecostal rivets of raw emotion. Pour through seams of empty thoughts. The sketches and etches of the outline of your heart, permeated deep into these sanctions of mine. In the emptiness of a devilish desire I contemplate the essence of this existence. Trances unwash themselves in the middle of the dwindling daylight hours. I poured heart after soul down my gleaming neck. In the grainy hope that one of them would bring me back to the light. In vacant glances and knowing eyes I see the infinite stars as they ponder my mortality and entice me with visions of lives that will never be, and there you are, the silent soul that flows through my memories. There you are the seraphic emptiness that kisses the top of my lip like fire coated salutations and gleaming, streaming echoes of my own bitter enticing emotions, all the words that will never be will still be, something more than this.

Making sense in the unrest between the wanting of my soul and the beating of my tampered heart. The eyes see which translates colours to my mind which sends emotions to my heart. But what if there is more, what if behind the light there exists some other kind of world that these discontented eyes have not been trained to see. There is no sense in war. There is no way to comprehend this anger that humans are taught to feel. There is no pleasure in hurt and if only we could learn to divert the attention of our consciousness to love. I race away with slivers of nothing. Trying to gain something other than what the news wants me to believe. There is more love then hate. I sift through ancient texts in hope that it will reveal something about my future. I believe in everything and everything needs to be real in the chimera state as well as this waking reflection we call life.

My heart falls. Like empty words between the spaces that stop. Then start. Then stop again. In the fevered echoes of hallucinations, we glide through eternity with desire pouring out of our eyes like crystal jewels that glisten in the burning sun and burning like traces of raw emotions that haunt the stirring hours like December ghosts. In other worlds I deliberated on the secrets of your soul, for all of time and space I am merely a disciple of my fiery heart and a slave to my glowing imagination which devours your presence like a thief in the night and each night just a second before I fall asleep, the whole of your existence flashes before my eyes and for that one brief moment the eternal fires of lust punish the ground I walk on and taunt me with the scent of your perfume which I cant escape from in this life or the next. So until the sun falls we fight on through the ash and breathe again and again. Until everything becomes nothing just like the shadows in my ether.

I chase you. In the wallowing crevices of my visions. You occur like sentimental edges of my rapture, drenched in your scent and burning holes of want with your elegance. My fevered breath. My bated words that appear before my eyes like a rehearsed play that was written before words began, in the empty hours that fickle like a candle flame, just the touch of your energy sends earth quakes of passion through my veins that deliver blood to my pulsating heart that beats and skips then beats again and again for you. When your lips taste mine the levels of ecstasy that drowns my consciousness, overshadows every second that I erased from the watch of time when you weren't mine. But now you imbue my eyes with everlasting grace and feelings that my yearning rapaciousness have no names for and many never will. So from here until the end of time I'll chase you in my soul.

Eyes that see through the façade of hope. Bitter words that curse through the glimmers of perfection that co exist and don't exist all in the same shadow, standing on the verge of my sanctions I see past realms of this reality and in my visions I play the part of a drunken fool. Stumbling my way in and out of this reality. There is never any right or wrong just explanations that we use to justify and fuel our dark propensity that swallow our morals in the fraction of a second, in an instant when all our wants and visions of lust, lose themselves in a wave of angelic halos that caress the inner voice. Plagued by the theory of mortality, death lurks behind times. The silent shawl. The opulent emotion, in the words of many men, many great souls that left their spirits in music and in prose. I salute the minds and fevered feelings that were left waiting for me to find. The world is a smaller place, whispers have become modern day screams. Day has turned to night and everything happens and is gone in the seconds that hold us back. That hold the floodgates of our drenched hunger that threatens to pour out of our souls and each day it rises until it breaks through and we are true to the inner callings of the spirit. We will be free to see reality for what it is in our subconscious, through pure eyes and hearts and feelings that we can control and will one day understand.

You drift off into my semiconsciousness state. An apparition of turmoil and with just one glance from your opulent eyes you bewitch me into a state of something. A state of want that has no name. it happens so suddenly. The yearning of my pulse. The burning of my skin to be near yours. In the dead of night these cravings project through to the other worlds. In dilemmas of sentimental excitement I glance through other avenues in the hope that this passion will extinguish itself into the slivers of tomorrow but right now this is no ordinary situation.

Slight hands. Scented words. Playing out the roles. Forgetting with each second a bit more of yesterdays dreams. This right here. It exists. It breathes it thinks and all the while I continue and walk through grey streets forgetting one more word, one more gesture that I once had.

Memories project on the walls of my white canvas mind. Moments that connected like transparent crevices of light. White on white. I died more times than I could count. We all shed skin and more and more we are one moment closer to the immortal world.

And during the haze, I woke up surprised that I was still here, my world blurred around me, spun out of any sense of order. My beliefs rose and wandered aimlessly off the shore and away from any realness. False idols, false people, false days that never ended. After all the fighting, doubting, misdirection I'm still here fighting once more. Thoughts pushed down onto my mind like thousands of years of worries. My eyes closed and hallucinations became a little bit more then dreams. I could walk forever and not really care. But in life we stick to familiar paths. We dabble in new surroundings and sometimes the words that you think about wont come out at the right time. Sometimes the doubt you feel is so real that you think you might not breathe again, and death waits behind each corner. This spirit it feels with parts of my soul, it wakes up and washes the sleep from its eyes. Surroundings can fit everything in, compress the air and figure out how to keep on breathing. We send emails and the details of our lives get lost in someone elses hard drive. We all can be so much more than we are. There has to be more emotion, more feeling, more and more of what we think we many never find. So beneath all the hardship, we struggle to make sense of all the objects and labels that dissect all that is around us. Every little tiny broken detail labelled like scientists and fair-haired echoes. The words never stop flowing. The pictures never stop getting labelled, mesmerised like forgotten words. We fight on and remain strong like we always will be.

Pictureless vestiges. You feel. Hear. See. Words pour out of shallow thoughts, mind tick tocking, clocking in and out of ancient dreams. Sleep walk through the initial frail soft moments that strengthen and turnover emotions. The sun sets later, but it never does really set. We see it rise and glide over the waves of doubt that we once had once felt. Picture and captured words cheapen the moment. Labels take away the true meaning of what this really is. Does anyone ever really know? Are we really capable of understanding? It never really goes anywhere. As we walk away it dissolves, but we see it again and again and again. Memories play out like drunk seconds remembered in the daylight. The sun wakes everything up, you, us. The night gets lost, then found. They balance and we have no resistance we can trust and we let things be, free.

Incandescent lights. This waking world is full of mortals with engulfed mesmerizing emotions. Subsiding into the outer realms. Fragrant moments of subdued passion. Lift off and take flight amongst curious eyes and unfettered hearts. Everything needs to be something. Sometimes words can not convey exactly what is real. Burnt out eagerness plagues minds and weary hearts. Are we ever really not bound by chains? Are we ever really free to be who we really are? Lost ships of poignant fervour. Lost hearts and empty voices. Caressing the edges of this so called reality. We walk streets and cast lights over dark walls, or is it the other way around? Searching for glimpses of our souls. It never really ever makes sense. All these borders and boundaries. In the end, we can not pretend that anything other than love ever really meant anything at all.

Hoping for anything more than this here. Pictures overlap in some other time. The minutes between night and day, awake and sleep. Contrived and the gaps grow smaller and smaller, these bodies, we separate our minds from our bodies. One controls the other. Is there ever really a point to any of this? I wake up and feel like this part is the truth. Then I sleep and live the alternate state. This life we are always bound by chains. Chains of emotions, chains of physical weight that push our bodies and level our energies into desperate emotions that control the essence of our being. I never wanted any of these worlds to be real. I never wanted any of these worlds to lock me down. We move across land. We design machines and make so many objects that are so much stronger than ourselves. The world is one big designer shopping mall. We spend the dwindling hours holding shopping bags filled with unwanted objects, each one taking a little more room in our empty souls. We are so much more than this, there is life in life. We choose to get caught up in all the moments that in the end don't mean anything at all. We walk the quiet streets in the night arms crossed to keep out the cold, arms crossed to keep out the forgotten devotions, arms crossed to keep out the world from entering through our feeble chests, born into this. Co existing. There is so much fight in these hearts. The beatnik free spirit caught in a consumers kingdom. So many have never really opened their eyes, so much to do yet so little time. We play the game but most of us don't even know the rules. Some win, some lose, we are always one moment away from winning all of it and one nano second away from losing everything we ever thought we knew about this life. It all rests on the shores of another place that has no name, no concept of who we even are and no notion of anything but life itself.

Hesitant ideals that hang from the tears of tomorrow. De ja vu like joy division. Melodic transparent fires that lose themselves time and time again. The everyday fades away, banal activities that don't really do anything else but fly away with the night. Words formulate and we procrastinate towards one more chance at freedom deep dreams that take the whole waking day to forget about. This life is attainable then it disappears across the horizon of another lovers lips. See through the canvas. The white shades of another's hopes. We deconstruct people and construct notions of lost love. Its easier to hang in the past. To recite salutations and stories that are so familiar. We mourn days and moments. We mourn the loss of seconds that never come back or get another chance. We spend hours begging for other days, other places and faces that have no meaning to right now. We pay our lives away on plastic cards that turn materialistic fantasies into more objects that take up more space than we really have. We have to buy land and houses we don't even want. We drive cars we don't need and just accept that two and a half men is the most watched show in the world. This life it plays out in the back lit rooms of seedy bars. With nameless characters that will never be named and found. It all rests in the ether of time. Without love we are nothing but shells.

It bitterly rests on the tips of yesterday. People parade in the shadows of themselves. Blind and buried beneath idols that they don't even know. The beginning of the start. Too many lost souls walking around like comatose vessels. It never really matters. Grey haired women with band aid knees and short socks. Walk down grey streets with grey eyes. Empty faces sit in silence next to lost other faces, only inches apart but light years away in spirit. This life is meant to grind you down. But we need to participate wait and sleep and only come back for more. No sanity just erratic letters of past lovers locked in sordid memories that flash by like flames of lost winters youth, people sitting next to nothing. Imagining moments that disappear as quickly and as sordid as they appear. If we should met in other universes we would never know as it wouldn't feel like it ever really happened at all. Layers upon layers upon unravelling secrets that open and close like words that we never ever said, chasing objects of lust that vanish the very instant they try and become permanent. We are only residue of who we thought we would be. Until the eyes open and see it for what it really is. There is no divide only borders that we are meant to put around ourselves. It all matters in the end. Every single breath matters, for the one we miss, we'll never breath again.

Tethered bitter emotions. Portrayed beneath the rocks of time. It encounters shallow waves that wash over ideals. Years take only days to pass. Days that creep past like swollen shadows. I encountered serpents instilled in tumultuous moments of hesitation. These words pour out and poured in are reflections of serpentine phantasms that fight so hard to stay alive. Bitterness that twists this body is stronger and more vivid then the outside walls. We create walls to separate us from them but are we all not the same? The same breath, the same beings, the distractions formulate and we procrastinate like beggars in the rain and the system exposes all our hopeless desires that burn the light, faded seraphic traces of yesterdays tears. We travel on this road. Destined by families and names of fortified saints who want to rule a world that will one day exist no longer. The resources run scarce and what you want is to hold the world in the palm of your hands until it all turns to grit. No more emptiness and feelings of isolation. We create worlds in every second of everyday and we are always here to stay.

It's a vessel. Spectres torment the waking hours where reality overcomes the shadows or tomorrows goodbyes. Controlling the destiny of more than we know. The whole system designed to distract. Distract from the truth. Everything is designed to consume and spend. The whole system conspired to make us associate belongings to souls. The exterior, a reflection of the interior. But if we don't know the inside then the other is surrounded by a false sense of tortured objects that reflect not who we are but actually what the system wants us to be. We judge and feel false senses of desires which we have conditioned to bank accounts and cyberspace we watch brain numbing television. The Prozac of the masses. We spend our lives playing sport watching sport. When we're not consuming we are wasting time and obstructing from the reality that certain Gods rule this world. They watch us, they don't fear us. They put people that have been designated and we read magazines about celebrities babies. We cant escape from the materialistic reality and we take 20 year mortgages, the great Australian dream is really a nightmare. We're not free, we work 40 hours a week to pay debts, we associate with people we don't like and we lie and cheat and con our way into lives and clubs. Many people spend more money on drugs and alcohol, asleep to what they really are. Drugs, crime only exists because we chase God through rolled up paper notes. Alcohol kills, cigarettes kill. But they're legalised so we drink when we are happy, we blow out the realness and associate reality stars with who we really are. Its status. We do it to impress people we don't like or don't even know. Separate entities and contort the truth. Dharma is man made. We only want to know who we really are. We live in the past, die in the future. We take ownership of people like they can be owned we have given everything a price, but in doing that we have lost the value of everything, even our soul is translated to a dollar sign.

So long it goes without the whimper of your name. I swayed in the twilight because I felt that this moment wasn't worthy enough for the both of us. I swayed as we lay there without a care. The television in the background a background show that wasn't even worthy of our attention. The telephone was lost to our ears and the notions of time were not exactly as they ought to have been. I hadn't seen what I wanted to, I hadn't known anything greater then that feeling of belonging to something greater then myself. Every time someone like you got close I pushed away because trust and fairness are two instruments that I forgot how to play along the way to where I am right now.

Back water bandits confide in telepathic scents of mild welfare. The train carries souls through tunnels, eyes stare blankly out into the carriage, smells of soap, aftershave and perfume. Heads nod and lips smile, a hundred minds saturating their auras with thoughts of yesterday, tomorrow and next year. Right now a hundred realities co-exist with desire, hope and dreams, falling out like tears on a young girls placid cheek. The earphones in my ears block out the sounds and we ride on a Tuesday morning though grey clouds that ponder above our heads. There is no other moment but right now, right now as I write these words and stare into sets of eyes that stare back at me. The train stops, I step out into the fluorescent underground passageways, man made waterfalls and escalators and elevators that take us to other realms as I walk with wandering eyes and tired steps and immaculate feelings. I participate and co operate with the rules and regulations. A smile says so much there is a sanity in all the madness, there is an energy that surrounds us and our thoughts permanently. It was never going to be better or easy, the days forge their way into my dreams I chase someone down stairs that are vaguely familiar, thoughts come and go like singing halo's in October, so much has happened yet the rain drops keep falling from the clouds and as this year nearly ends and another starts I find solitude in knowing that my words always rang out the truth if I ever said what I didn't mean then my words said the opposite, I rectified my sanctions and burnt holes in your voice, your voice which will fade into nothing but a silent whisper and you who will succumb to the transparent feelings and people that will have no idea what it is you are and what it is we almost had.

I chase you. In the wallowing crevices of my dreams. You occur like saccharine edges of my desires. Drenched in your scent and burning holes of want with your elegance, my fevered breath. My bated words a rehearsed play that was written before time began. In the empty hours that fickle like a candle flame, just the touch of your energy sends earthquakes of passion through my veins that deliver blood to my pulsating heart that beats and skips, then beats again for you. When your lips taste mine the levels of ecstasy that drowns my consciousness, overshadows every second that I erased from the watch of time, when you were not mine. But now you infiltrate my eyes with ever lasting grace and feelings that my yearning desires have no names for and may never will. So from here until the end of time, I'll chase you like rainbows in my dreams..

One summer I pondered the realms of your chastity. Do you remember that day? My birthday. I drove to your work. It was hot. But the failing feelings I felt took over my being like a drug fuelled frenzy in a dirty alley way. Every atom in my body panicked the second you came near me, like my feelings were an actual entity, one that other people could see from afar. Words rushed out of my mind but somewhere along the way to my mouth they got lost. Forgotten. So I stayed silent you taking me to be the guy with nothing to say, but really I wrote poem after poem about how you made me feel. And it wasn't just a feeling. It was more. The very second our lips met I chased rainbows in my thoughts. We kissed by the side of the road, cars passed, each one signifying a feeling of want that I felt, of gratitude to every God that this moment was real and just. You felt it too, our lips locked and played, together. The words our eyes spoke were sent directly to the epicentres of our souls. So young in age but I knew that in past lives I savoured you. Like right now. Everything you didn't say was enough for as I held your head and the tips of our fingers searched for solace in each others skin; I never wanted to hear your voice again. I lost myself in a moment; I surrendered to the fabricated thoughts that journeyed to my being. It was hot. I remember. I remember the gentleness of your touch, your smile after every pause in our kiss. The way your hair ran through my hands and we weren't standing there, for that moment we languished and touched and rose to the sanctions of the sky, where lightning strikes and clouds were born and remembered. On your lunch break. A break from the world, you wrote your name with every vein in my body. For years on end my heart beat on grey streets for you to come back, but you went away. You couldn't stay and every day I spoke the ears off helpless victims whose only crime was to ask me how I was feeling and how I was sad. Sad that you left. That day we kissed kept me going and in every girls eyes I searched for you in disguise. There was no one thing that I could define. You just had something that I needed that felt normal and justified when you were near me. Like my life was black and white until you made it colour. You left and my feelings subsided to journals and stories, I listened to Sade and the Cure and I knew I wasn't alone. For 3 years you vanished. The one and only letter you sent from a stony Mediterranean island I kept in a cigar box under my bed, and then I forgot about you the very second I heard you were back.

And my heart stopped the second I heard. We met and made love and there was something missing in your eyes and in my words. We made passionate love on cars in summer. No place was too sacred for our yearning desires. The world was ours and nothing existed but that moment. Lust, passion, fire, turmoil. It was our own movie one where we wrote the scenes and you still wore the necklace I gave you. And nothing mattered. But time had dampened our feelings. Slightly. Something was a miss. Then I moved on, I wandered streets alone and found scents of other women more intimate then our crumbling feelings. Years passed I searched the world with other hearts and you became a memory. I thought about you and wandered if you were ok. And I shouldn't have but I did and it was something I had no control over, then I came back and one morning she left me and all I could think of was you. And I wanted to call you but didn't then that very day as I stammered around Melbourne streets staring at other faces as I held it all together I went to work and you walked in. You walked in like an apparition in the December sunlight, you walked up to me and I froze. And you told me that the following day you were getting married and that word hit me like a chastised bullet, as I knew we were saying goodbye forever. That word, the final closing of the door between our hearts at the end of a corridor called time. And in time you seemed to vanish from my mind, like a sentimental memory that diluted and diluted until you finally became the epitome of dust, and so it ended just like it begun...time and time again...

My mind wanders through selected states of reality. Formulated words and in my dreams seraphs chase me. Girls swim with me with crystal coloured eyes and I beckon carnival rides and ride motorbikes and follow women over seas of darkness, two sisters call my name and I fight hooligans and smash in heads and get chased. Then I wake and I don't know which world is more real. I don't know which life I need to follow. The deeper meanings, the hesitation. The lucid mess the quest to fulfil desires that can never be filled as much as we try, it can never be satisfied. The insatiable desires, the turmoil of not being in control. It hurts and the helplessness, the burning feelings to become something other than who we are. To transform the consciousness into hot embers of this world. All my life I asked questions about situations that I knew nothing about. Putting my trust and hope into ideals and hearts that didn't even know my name. There has to be something more than this. Un-abiding quests and people walking around parading in alleyways that they have never really seen before. Standing on the edge. In order for someone to love me first I must love myself. From all sides I feel it pushing me, its getting tighter and I'm trying my hardest to keep it all sane and free from the darkness that eludes the sunlight of my dawn.

Jaded drops of perfection, wash down your eyes to mine. Our time together, a thousand dreams, melted into one aura of delight, your words take flight and our bodies intertwine into surreal symbols of ancient Archangels. Our bodies fit together in ways that our lips do. Our words resonate like lost echoes of bewildered lust that beats this heart of mine. And the second our lips touch for the first time, every time I reach places of ecstasy that I never knew were real. I feel like you being in my arms is the moment when time stands still and our breathing is in sync. They are moments that reach out and capture the essence of why I am here and the very second I ever laid eyes on you somewhere voices sang and my heart spoke words that only now I vaguely understand. It told me that maybe just maybe it was all meant to be. In the summer we kiss in the winter we hold each other to keep warm you and I, you and I , every breath I take speaks to me your name. it's never the same the world belongs to you and I, it always will, cant you see? Its all meant to be.

Tick tocking immortal trails of yesterday. Smashed between the pinnacles of loneliness. Loveliness, the next best thing to eternity. Existing in waves of pleasure. We see, we try to conquer and devastate our morals with one sentence, thoughts play out and we are only subjects that will one day be studied some time away. wandering, breathing, being. The nouns all mount up into one big novel of hope, ecstasy merges with memory to bring a simple smile into this cloudy day. Decisions wait around substitute corners of hope we are all invincible in the end. One email away, one text away from finding freedom. The physical part of us, who we are has nothing but freedom attached. We are all creatures of the sun and moon. Nothing is here unless we make it here. Nothing breathes until we feel its pulse. Cascading in and out of dreams. People mouths open for words to come out but what comes out aren't words but symbols of love disguised as thoughts but in the end we are all chasing the same ideals just in different ways. We are all permanent like stars. Millions of souls, billions of years old. Crushing on the rocks of understanding we slide away, then crash back on the shore. Some thoughts come easier, gliding, riding, biding the time ticks away like sailing notions of want and lust. There is no such thing as pain. Only want and elegance and cosmic feelings of tenderness. We caste away the bad, we all want to be held. Somewhere existing are other stronger parts of us. All sped out and lost in the umbrage. We feel things our mind cant comprehend,

we feel feelings that have no origins or words and worlds
are not enough, eyes only say so much. This poem could go
on and on but its in the verse that hasn't been written that
means more that will come when it comes when its begun,
for we are all one.

The sun creeps its shady hands above the rising sketches of the day, the chimeras wash itself away with the opening of my eyes, all that I have ever been is lost the second this sad reality comes into focus. In the waking hours the soul and the body play out these games, the cat and mouse, the sinner and the sinned. The future casts innervated shadows over the afterglow we are and always will be who we are the sound of our voice the colour of our eyes. Its never enough, the desire for more overshadows the will to be free. Possibilities play out like over cumbersome day dreams from long ago. Each day that passed creeps up the mind like tiny over shaped diamonds that need to be seen to be believed. The atrocity of never knowing the truth. Over sized men in oversized rooms talk with fire in their words and the devils tongue. Absoluteness on the streets, it all means the same thing when you break it down. Speculate that my name isn't my name that it only came after me. Not chosen by me. That's a word that too many don't dare to think about. Something is going on, something is always going on somewhere, and we never really know who we are or what our real name really is.

Forgotten traces of your slender words. I trampled on past times and lost loves and I failed to see the truth. I visited our favourite places and as I sipped on cheap coffee and reminisced about your vogue lips. I watched you there again but again the idea of you was so much stronger then the actual you. Its when you're not here that my mind travels across lifetimes to salvage you. Its when you're with me that I cringe and wait for you to say words that I wish would translate and appear like hallucinations out of your mouth, but they don't and instead you only worry about yourself. You don't like hearing the truth as if the truth is a blanket that you have put away, you're scared of your own feelings, but you are like me in the same way that you can be in the moment and not care about the consequences. I can live without you I can move on its just that after so long of staring candidly into soulless eyes I felt something with you. But for every indication that you feel the same which I don't doubt you close it off and don't care about how I would feel you take things for granted you chase attention like I chased you and in doing that you may have lost the only soul that could ever love you with no boundaries, no limits and no rules.

My words resonate into darkness and this cold weather seeps its way into me again and again but I fight on. I have a way of forgetting about the things I have already done. And I hope that you will someday be more than a memory.

Bitter scotch accents and peticured dreams. They over lap across waves of light and constantly we search for that glimmering light of hope. I chase dimness across indistinct lanes. And the torment that you're not here plagues these words and something else. Something so much more. The piano plays songs of past loves that fall through the notes like leaves in autumn. Falling and falling. It is actually you that I really want. Or am I chasing luminous states of myself. Chasing feelings and words that you can never say or give me. If I look back on the months that our passion was born that wept on my delusions like ghosts in a backwater southern town, I have the intuition that maybe just like yesterday I've been living in a lucid dream one where you are as good as I think you can be, this reality transforms. I chase houses and bars of gold in my dreams. People I don't know talk to me about places I've never been but I feel like I have. Each morning I arise. the shards of light reflect on the emptiness of my desire and protrude through the sheeting blinds, the sounds of outside forge their way into this room and I lay there motionless wondering exactly what it is I have been doing who it is I have been intoxicating with and where all the time and patience went. The days merge into one I'm transfixed and tired just trying to make sense of it all.

I sold snippets of our time together to heartless souls that slid their way into vague rooms with eyes that beckoned to have only a fraction of passion that I washed in oceans of you. It was right there all along, glimmering like a constant ray of the sun, your voice resonated across foreign lands and I only ever whispered the truth in your slender ear, when you lay next to me all those nights and mornings that spiritually we travelled to universes that have yet to even be dared to be born. You gave me a feeling that had no words or sound. Your eyes transported me to a place that you didn't even know about. The tragic poet became a king just by one movement of your tongue which conquered my bitterness. You weren't even aware of your own beauty but that was what made you real. Since I was old enough to understand the words I wrote I chased feelings that I pondered as an old soul I embattled the echoes of your tears and I devoured the sentiments of our eternal love.

Men with two dollar bottles of wine salvage the remaining minutes of sunlight like hyenas running wild. The sun steals the warmth then it transpires and it creeps away like ravens flying floating through the air. Eyes wander past me, semi conscious souls bordering on the brink of reality. People sit in parks with parkas and solidified moments of solitude. Women dressed not to flatter anything but only to obstruct the scenery with opulent dresses that hurt my eyes. Foreigners sell objects that resemble plastic cards but really they spawn evil actions. So many people barely not even breathing. Not even bothering to ask questions that will bring them new thoughts. The lazy minds watch formulated television about lives and affairs and people that don't care anymore than the authorities do. People sit in trams and talk on metal objects. Revealing all their grit for the world to hear. People have to stop thinking that anyone cares about them as much as they care about themselves.

It comes to me. The lucid memories of you. Time its ruthless it's unforgiving. Situations that I find myself in right now I never asked for them. But the reality of my waking days were over rode by my dreams. For the longest time I had no consequence or care for myself. Looking back now I realised that I didn't really care about the future. I wanted to surround myself with the drunkard walls and cocaine frenzied fevers, for when the waves came I washed myself away. They took me to parts of the sea that were not tainted by other peoples lives and problems. The course of my life flew out of control. So out of touch with myself that at some stage I forgot who I really was. I travelled half way across the world to discover what I already knew. For some reason I cared too much about other peoples opinions of me. The exterior became the focus but inside and around I wreaked a small havoc. Like a thunderous hurricane. My priorities formulated and my own self doubt took control. I felt like a bystander in the scene of my life. My past has hurt me, so now I stand alone the future turns away and I must make the wrong right again. The answer to my problems lies with myself I need to take control and live out my destiny.

In my dreams I chase demons across desert plains. The epicure of my happiness holds itself in the mellow hours. This shell of mine this body it feels like the wrath of Godless plays that I starred in for so many years. What I thought was the reason for my being was a distraction I forged ideals that washed away my purpose. Washed away like a child playing by the river of my solace. I indulged in women who transpired into my being, women who gave me nothing but words that I tried to decipher in my head and pour out onto this page. Reality and dreams crossed over, hollowed landscapes of my emptiness. I thought I lost myself and I did, looking in the mirror I was unaware of the face looking back at me. Like it was another face not my own. If my life was a star I got lost in the white light and now I am only being found again. I neglected the real reasons why I was here. I sat in cafes around the world just sipping caffeine trying to make sense of this world and the more I tried the less I thought about who I was.

I've been a beatnik living in a materialistic world for way too long thinking that I have been someone else. But this is me this is who I am and the person is only just being born. Other people are nothing but jaded words. If I listen to everyone else all the time then I wont get anywhere. I have created a situation for myself and now I'll make it right again.

Two dollar wine poets hang in the shade of ancient churches. The sun rests its fainted head between the cracks. Surrounded by bated breaths and red cars that divide the road. Tram bells ringing, the big issue man singing. People drink red wine, head in iphones and of all the places we can be we are here, and beer flows through shady gutters and all these realities co exist. Above the clouds like desperate shapes of anguish we glide through the dry and drink coffees and talk about the way we want it to be, and the sureness of what it really is. My mind wanders through the paths of the past, locked up are the moments and there's been many greater and more significant then this. Everywhere I stand, wherever I go I have to remember that this could be the last time and it is the last time because these moments indeed never happen again and I cant pretend that I care more than I do. Why do we fight the great fight? What more is there to obtain? Are well all not reflections of dreams. Situations dictate events and for a third of my life I left my soul on bar stools and bedrooms that passed by like servants serving their masters in ancient Egypt. I only wanted to be the poet. The lover. The gentle fragile soul that I harnessed on tear shaped desires that fell through my fingers like sand. Washed out and isolated from the vulnerable reality that lost itself in moments of time that hung on walls of yesterday. Our bodies are shells, and the outward world unhinged its way into my psyche. I got used to the idea of de ja vu like an energy I could reach out to and hold with the edges of my fingers. I stammered my way through serious waves of procrastination, I salvaged words like a hangover, lying in sketches of soberness. I was drunk so many times that being jaded became a normality. Dry lips and an unquenchable thirst for something other than myself ensured. I fell to the vices. The system became the law and I lost myself so many times that vagueness was an ideal that I swore by, I never wanted any of this, I never asked for anything In a voice louder then a whisper. My heart ache and yearning for someone to understand was just another thought that crossed my mind like broken pencils in primary school. The dream state overlapped with the waking world, and I travelled across the world to find an answer to a question I wrote and hid in my bedroom at home. I chased girls that I ran from the minute I showed my true self because somehow I was afraid of the person I didn't want to be. I watched others around me fall into states of instant gratification. Tomorrow never existed. The pain caused was something that being invincible never even mattered. I washed money down the drains of bars and the mouths of second hand dealers. I fed egos and found solitude in the moments I wanted to erase. When the music stopped and I saw myself in dusty mirrors I realised that the person looking back was someone I didn't really know, I focused on the other realms and places I thought I wanted to be. Its easy to fall for the vices and salutations of other peoples romances about what this life is meant to be. I remained quiet when I wanted to shout. I went along with journeys and I preached about guru's that I knew better then to follow. It all makes sense and as intense as it is. There 's always right now to make the wrong right again. A thousand possibilities exist on every second of every day. The train of thought parades through my mind and the closer I am the more sanity I find to be true to who I am. To stand up and inspire and transpire through the streets and clouds of denial. There is no trial in the end, its only the consequence of right now and I can't be someone else. Because no one else is more significant and nothing means more then making the most. We are all hosts and this right here is here because I am here, so what I choose win or lose is always right as long as I feel the light of the sun overshadow the wrong and it's a new day and the sun is here to stay and yesterday is a song whose words remain permeated across hearts and souls that strive to find a certain peace of mind. Decisions glide through echoes of this day and in every other way we are always here to stay.

I lost myself. I tracked through valleys of your distrust. As we sat by the window I left avenues of your words in messy segments of my mind. Laid out before me like a premonition of lost love. In other lifetimes I wandered around castles hoping to disguise myself as something more than I already was. I trapped myself in hollow fractions of my mind. My reality a formulated spell revolving around your fake empty self. I chased a feeling that you couldn't give me, which was layered with corners of my soul. As I opened my eyes in the morning I forgot about the lies that you wanted me to believe. I never said anything more then what I meant or wanted you to think. I saw myself in every waking moment. Me standing next to myself, listening to words that I wanted to try and disguise. It never came easy, I wish you had let yourself surrender to the feelings that you shared only it was never enough, my feelings were never enough for you, and caste out like a sleepless restless soul I pondered the remnants of your shell, for the rest of time.

That November night brandished us, it over took desires and turned the turmoil into pleasant feelings, that we accepted as the truth we didn't need other faces or names or energies, the night played out like scenes from another time, another land. The days turned to months, my new muse was born and you took my feelings to heights that the others had only pondered. I didn't want to accept it, that it was here and I had to just say ok I get it now, after so long of swimming in cold waters that were shallow and fragile I found the ocean that I had always wanted to find. The factors of my life, I realised that I was running away for so long, running from the person I wanted to be and the career that I needed to take, always wanting the easy way out, always worrying about the moment and never tomorrow, I was doing anything I could to escape my reality, and just before you arrived I had made some decisions that were going to change the course of my life, do I stay and just keep wallowing on the surface, not even pushing further just taking anything that came my way? Or do I go out into this amazing world and take the destiny that awaited me all along?

As I stopped the substitutes and the tools of escape I saw my stance for what it was and it scared me and throughout all this time you were there at the right time you made me believe in resonances and feelings that I thought I would never feel again, you summed up how I felt with just the way you looked at me and every kiss we ever shared, every word

I ever whispered to you when we were alone I meant, apart from the times when I was mad at myself and the bearings of our desires, I played the part of a fool that was never me but became me to protect myself and to stop doubting what it was that I was and what it was that we found. My travels and direction right now are the hardest I've ever had to face, it hurts to be alone in the cold in a city that doesn't care about me, it hurts that you don't care enough to even see if I'm ok, but I'm a long long way from home and to become who I need to be and to go further I must let go of the things that are my past.

I see my reality now without any altercations without any substances to distort the truth some of it is a brutal truth while other things are amazing. My ups are high and my downs are the worst I've ever felt, I feel the old me fading a little, people and places I remember and they will always be with me, I deleted every message you sent only subtle reminders of the way you felt not feel now. I've never known the feeling of being complete by just sitting on a bench in a busy street, I never knew the genuine intensity of what it was to be in another world when being intimate like it always was with you, I know that I'll never find that again, I don't think I ever want to, I left a part of me with you and you with me, that night or the nights at your car door, when the hot night wind blew shadows at our ears while we kissed under the moon, they are moments in time that I will freeze frame in my mind and whenever the cold hurts and the darkness overshadows and I'm alone and scared I'll think of those times and smile because no one and nothing can take that away from me. Everything reminds me of you; I write this all because it clears my head and makes me think of new things. Usually I'm so good to just forget, I'm so eager to walk away and move on but with you it's hard and it hurts but I must and it must mean something, so what now? I leave you my feelings with these words, what you decide, what you want, what it is you need I will accept, I've done enough and bled enough and now I really need to take in everything around me with new eyes that are not hindered by you and all the things I didn't say and whether or not I made the right choice and what if I had stayed? Because right now it's irrelevant. I'm here and this is my world and the rest waits and the stage is waiting and I will go to the next level now that I have no distractions and I'll think of you and your smile and all the other intricacies that make you you and make you amazing and unique and special.........

I wanted your love to drip, drop over me like a broken tap that just drips and drops its steady timed droplets into my being, I only wanted to hold you on the nights that I felt I could reach out and pause. Then kiss you. Then press play again. We lay there so many times, nurturing our love like fossils that were so delicate that if we breathed the wrong way we may have crumbled our sanctions in our fingers. I thought of you as easily as it was to be in your presence, what ever you had said, raced to the walls of my mind and tattooed themselves like graffiti in a dirty back water town. You opened up the other realms of space and time that were never there, I raced around cities just to catch a scent of your fragrance I built castles and fortresses around our days and nights together so no one in their right or un-right mind could ever wash them away. My lips are still scarred from your kisses, my ears are still ringing from the whispers that you privately and emotionally expanded with your sweet dialogue into my ear, and frozen are the portraits of us and the time that is sketched like a hieroglyph in an ancient pyramid, and as I wander these streets and see vintage cars and praying fiends and as the constant rain rains down onto me and cleanses my fire I think of you and every step I take is one more step between us, one more way in which no matter where we both are the invisible vices hold things together like gravity but not like it, like lust but so much more. There are feelings and places that exist because the two of us found them that have yet no names and they will always remain nameless and timeless and no matter what, where or when its not the big picture that matters but the tiny ways in which you made me yours and I without even knowing it made us one. Now and later I found myself, the second I lost it. I found you and then you left no sooner then you came and took my breath away. I never wanted to want you, I was full of resentment and resistance, not to you but to my feelings and situations, I wandered the streets in clouds of fog, I could only see a few feet ahead and through all that time I forgot who I was and doubted myself, you opened up the doors that I locked and walked past so many times trying to ignore them, I felt that if I pretended they weren't there then they weren't.

We spent so many nights unwashed and empty of anything else. The feeling you let suffuse into my being were as extravagant and mesmerising as anything I've ever known or felt prior or ever will. With one word from your gentle mouth you let me swim in your purity and just like the waters of the Mediterranean sea I just let myself be and it was a feeling I have yet been able to describe, I can now understand why I chose this way, I lost myself and it wasn't the first time I let it happen. The small intricate ways in which we are all special is a notion that I indulge in more often then I forget. All I wanted was honesty, unabashed decency and you. Nothing more, nothing less. The interaction we shared, I really think that in another lifetime we were inseparable like two peasants in a desert village, in a dry land where our love quenched our thirst and let the dry become nourished like water to fire. If I sit here I'll write for days on end without the need or thought for anything and anyone else. Just the memories of you and what it was we had and the feelings that came and went like the waves of that precious sea that I swam in that was you and your feelings and the way in which you looked at me with you auburn autumn eyes and I wanted nothing more then to lie there for years and soak up your aura until I was wrinkled and content.

The piano played tunes set in out cast loves and rays of the ocean glided by the window each and every time we pondered words and stories of you and I. I saw reflections of your shadow in down typed motives playing on the screen and I missed you.

I breathe deep breaths of the London cold air and I think about when it is I will see you again, my old life, and my new life now, I have shed skin so many times its hard to tell even for me when the new me begins and the old ones end. Its hard I'm not going to lie, hard like the time I wanted to tell you how I felt but couldn't, hard like the minute our good bye finally sunk in and it occurred for the very first time that it was actually going to be a while before we saw each other again, the distance between us we both knew that It would create waves and seas of forgetfulness and just as easily as I gave myself to you I hid it up again, kept it to me and walked away on that warm summer day to where I am right now, most of the hard part is over now, the settling in and finding my place once more is the biggest challenge, the thought of you and I just being has got me through many cold nights, I still haven't held a girl in the same way, maybe I'm scarred, maybe I'm afraid, maybe I'll feel that way again about you or someone else, I just don't know right now. I've never felt so solitary, so personified and determined to enter the next chapter of my life, I see who I was then and the person I am becoming and I know that it had to be this way, it hurts to be away from everyone and everything that means so much to me, but I am still on the mend, still finding my heart in streets that I wandered through so many years before today. I thought I knew you, then again I thought I knew myself, the heart ache turns to strength, my words resonate through the cold that still baffles and perplexes me, I dream of mountains and smiling faces, the enemy that was my alter ego has left and now stands the poet, the writer, the man that can do anything he likes whenever he likes on the road as it clears, I smile and wish you had chosen the way you really wanted to but you didn't and I'm here and you're not and I'm alone and you're not but its ok, we fight through another day and the thought of knowing that you were mine and those days and hours were ours alone is satisfying enough for now.....

Not to be forced but of course we already knew the ending came before the start. I walk the Hampstead streets, the cobbled stoned walls and floors I've been here before, sip on mint Moroccan tea, just me, and these thoughts and memories that lunge and plunge and take over my being, we remain in the present I am here now and you're there and as bare as the way our bodies lay together I remember that the hardest part was leaving you. There is a purpose a reason, is it treason if I see another girl and wander what it would be like to know her on a level as intimate and delicate as the way we were so many times before? These buses and streets and alley ways and lane ways, the travelling and pondering and this heart beats too my dear it beats for the return of that time we were one spirit dignified and personified into one aura of delight and as these thoughts take flight on another journey that swoops across my mind again, I pretend that tomorrow you may come into my work or just might be waiting for me to come home, and home is a notion that loses its meaning, everyday that I'm away, I just want to be strong to align the lines that aren't aligned and through all this I might find exactly what you really mean to me, let it be, now just let it be and we'll see if its all fate, your voice on the phone, its so unique and I've never really been alone, so alone I stand and alone I walk thought these Hampstead streets, isolated and dissipated, the old man in the second hand bookstore, he smells of stale air and unshaven madness but he knows every book in its disordered state and I wait for the words of writers that carved paths in my psyche, that paved the way for me to attain something that meant more then myself, and as your voice resonates through the metal phone I place to my ear, I hear your voice and say to you what I'm feeling, you know me, you understand the depths of these words and in turn I will open up to you when the timing is right, now this de-ja vu' that walks through walls and clouds to find me I see that after all this time it was always you that cared and spared the time to make me realise that life can be what we want it to be, we must stand and fight the battle its never easy and every feeling we have ever felt has been felt before, every situation that seems to have no conclusion its been felt somewhere else and in the context of my life my worries are insignificant as opposed to somewhere and someone else right now. I was never a weekend poet just a man with words on his mind, I sit now above the restaurant and the London blue sky spells out you name in vain time and time again.....

Dusty men parade through the streets like royal soldiers in July, I wander these streets, searching for who knows what, hell knows where, the cobbled street creeps under my feet and I'm on the hunt for something. I'm sure I just don't know what it is, white headphones and thoughts that circle through the sub way underground passages and tunnels lead to other tunnels and escalators that take us up passageways and alley ways, we make eye contact on the tube, she looks I look, she smiles I smile but no words come out, the chick, chick, chick of the train and I'm left speechless and then the doors open and she vanishes and the whole way home I think of all the other worlds of all the words that I wanted to say but couldn't wouldn't and won't ever get the chance to say to her, and then she's gone and only a memory left on this page, at this stage I should give it up but my heart beats more and more for that feeling of bliss, a kiss from her lips that reach out and warm up my body on this cold April day, it doesn't go away that flame that burns and we yearn for touches of ghosts that have no inhibitions that tell us they get us, they get this, they know what it is that is, and what is what and how its meant to be, but then maybe we never really know and I walk up hills and see my reflection in the shop windows of bookstores and fashion stores and people walk like its Sunday and it is Sunday and one day I wont walk alone anymore but right now when you want to write when you want to have no one to answer to its ok, because when you're alone you hear yourself and no one else. No whispers in your ear. No one to tell you anything you don't

want to know or don't want to disagree with, and the streets
as I walk I can't feel how tired I am in my legs because the
rush of being here just keeps me going and every stop I get
off at I feel like it's the first time I have been here, and its
all fresh and London has an energy that you can't really
touch but you feel it as you walk through Soho at 5pm when
the sun is out and you feel it when you walk on Regent
street and the swarms of people just keep swarming and if
you bend down to tie your laces you might just get walked
over, the beats of the city and heartbeats and bus stops and
grey skies then blues skies and grey walls and its mixture of
everything and anything and it's the gate way to the world
and I wouldn't want to be anywhere else right now and maybe
soon your reflection will be seen with mine as soon I build
up the courage to actually look at you and say what I want
to say without a hundred pairs of eyes watching me trying
to talk to you on a crowded tube at 7am, the timing is right
when its right and tonight we'll fight on and maybe we'll
see you in the morning or tomorrow or sometime then, but
until that day I can only hope that you're there somewhere
thinking of all the things you maybe wanted to say to me,
but we'll see, we'll just wait and see shall we?

I searched equators to find traces of you. I salvaged the inner sanctions of my being and when the timing was right and your trust was earned I let you in again and again into my world and all that I held sacred diminished with your first breath on my neck.

You paraded and caressed the inner thoughts of mine. As I rode through tubes and wandered into women who bit at my heels in search of peaceful words that I could unleash at any moment. You were the one that remained at the core of my existence. As I rode across places to foreign lands I spoke in whispers across the globe into your bedroom where you lay promising me that you were waiting for my return. I bought gifts and ideals and later as you lay next to me I poured out this heart of mine. And when the time came for you to show me in actions how you really felt you looked in the mirror and as you washed your face and ignored your feelings, you washed me away for good.

I never asked for more then what I gave. Your actions spoke volumes and the way you dealt with your situation was enough for me to know what you were really like. We are all Jekyll and Hydes, the smart, sweet caring likeable girl, then the selfish self-centered attention seeking one. I would like to sit here and believe that the real you was the one that I wanted you to be. I'll use this experience to become stronger and learn from your actions and mine. Soon enough if you

see through the façade of yourself you might realise what you
washed away, on a sunny day in August, one time, one moment,
one feeling one person that you let fade away............

It rained softly. Each drop reflected on the sandy surface of who I was. There were meagre feelings of anticipation that I fought so hard to not seep into my psyche. You wore shades of red that appeared to me like hallucinations and the turmoil I felt because I didn't have you hurt me in places and ways that I never wanted to know about. In every day we spent together I found portholes and gateways to other universes but for you it wasn't that hard or easy it was just another way, another place that you could shine and radiate just like you did before me and you will forever after. I was plagued by my insecurities and failing feelings of fragile peace. That twisted their way into my thoughts and words. But my actions were always louder, brighter and more significant then you could ever comprehend. We sat by the water it had stopped raining but the water kept falling inside washing away our energies. A smile a look it always meant something but being two people with two perspectives I took you for being an ageless beauty that I would fight so hard to keep and protect. But you were always looking for the next new rush, new experiences and loves and tragedies that you could never possess but only own for a fraction of a moment before it washed away like the waves at our feet as we sat by the ocean. I feel and you fell and birds of reason floundered and flew and I paid no attention to anything but my own selfish ways. I only wanted what I couldn't you only gave me what you shouldn't have. It started raining again and as heavy as the stones were that I held in order to stop holding you I remained silent. If only you could see the anguish, the turmoil that I concealed as I held stones and I accepted the truth that I could never hold you forever, a genius with words but a simpleton in love. You made me stutter and hesitate just by being in the same room, but as the days widened between our visits and kisses and love, I pondered the other portholes and women that were there all along but for the only reason that your star was brighter you caught my attention as easily as I caught a fever in winter called you. I only wanted to find perfection and what I found and lost with you was oh so close to that...........

You entice me but then you take it away. Words. We let them linger then drift off and we can't seem to find them again. Sometimes we can't even put them together in the same order, you spark a fire inside me, with one look of your eyes my fire burns bright then stays alight. You're almost as picturesque and as vivid as my memories and I would devour you for every minute of every day that we spend together if I could. The intensity prevails over what is right and what is wrong. In states of repetition in hours that dwindle and fly away my mind races up and down walls and each time it turns another corner it's you that comes to my mind. What it is we have we might never know. That feeling of belonging, comfort, serenity. It's something unlike anything else and it's beautiful and tragic and amazing and strong and windy and still.

That's all that should matter and to not want you would be to not want to live, it comes as easy and natural. That feeling of wanting that craving. The turmoil that turns into inspiration. The inspiration that keeps me sane and happy and blessed that I found you and you are in my life and no matter what or where that bond that language that we speak without talking will always be there. Amongst the sea of everything I found a diamond and just like a prized jewel I would love to keep you locked away but just like everything that exists that's as bright and rich and beautiful the world is a better place just because you're here and your smile could chase away a million demons and your kiss could ignite a million fires in the coldest of hearts, there is no substitute and every girl that comes after you couldn't hold a candle in your shadow, and I don't know why I feel this way about you its something you possess that I can see for what it really is and I wont forget it and I'll keep searching in every other girl for it but you could conquer worlds and inspire a thousand poems and never stop knowing that you are what you are and dolphins could with swim you and its all good and sacred and special and amazing...........

The feeble matters that meant so little at the time. I never wanted to be your patsi. The days, they were softer then your cheeks, cheeks that I caressed, your chest that burnt shallows of desire upon my bitter lips. I felt you solemnly, in the space of an instant, your thoughts were distant, who says rules had to be broken, that morning you know the one. The minute you hesitated I felt a kingdom somewhere in a far off land had collapsed. The relapse of your condition. My inhibition was easy to formulate you were always wiser then you wanted me to believe. When you closed your eyes I spoke to you of possible encounters that we might share. The laws of attraction brought us together, the laws of stupidity forced it apart. That afternoon as we lay, some would say you whispered words that made no sense, if only you could grasp the notion of infinity. If only you could have let the ghosts and the pain remain just that, I could have caressed that beautiful spirit of yours for hours, my words were more then letters joined to make something up it was more like my soul was saying something our minds didn't comprehend. The tears of your goodbye, hung on the corner of your eye for just a fraction longer it lingered for some unknown reason, your treason was my excuse to leave you, my reasons for accepting you outweighed the reasons why I shouldn't have. This life you know, it only consists of this moment, time is a segmented villain who taunts my sleep in the hollow hours of a summers night. Either right now this instant we take flight on another quest. My eyes embattle this very moment, I always tried my best. I gave you what I could, you stole kisses and glances, whenever we were together everything faded into the background, it enveloped the purity and blinded the touch of your body against mine. I'll be fine and so will you, we'll battle this existence, your tongue my only weakness. Greater men then I have died for less than this so now we'll float and glide through this moment. You always told me to stop dreaming, you words they were never known for their meaning.......

Speak to me. I'm so tried of talking that I only want to indulge in the language that has no vowels, verbs or nouns. We speak. Talk. Converse. But our words are they not just reverberations of our tongues, formulated to make meaning of every object, every feeling, every emotion and every moment?

Me right now, this page is only an interpretation of feelings that I know of no other way to explain.

Let me sit there by the window and watch you as you sit by me. Do I really need to say something right now, or does the look in my eye portray to you something else? Something real? Because right now I cannot tell you in words how much you really mean to me. Every moment we shared is somewhere behind these eyes of mine. Every coffee, every time we made love, it's here and behind your eyes where it lays peaceful and beautiful forever. You are the only one that can make me melt, that takes away my fears and lets me languish in my new memories, that passes us by like sheets hanging out to dry in summer. I'll let my eyes speak the language that my head or mouth can not decipher. That you know, because you know me so well and I'll experience every waking moment with new eyes and new thoughts of you and us and everything else that means something.

Inside and outside I suffocated the words that would have salvaged what we couldn't hold onto. My mind it constantly searches for clarity I've found myself in situations that I always wanted to be in and hidden in the crevices of my desire were glimpses of you. I listened to the CD you gave me and it saved me from the vices that opened and closed, opened and closed like my emotions and feelings towards you. The shutter was closed on the window that looked out onto the city where we met and found each other. Our souls could have met in other lifetimes, in other lands. I had never felt so alive and if I could sing I would have sang until my heart bled. I would have conquered worlds to know that you were safe and would be waiting for me upon my return. A calm overcomes me when you are near, and my heart beats irregularly until I get to a point where if we don't kiss I might stop breathing. Only for a moment, then I'll fall into that state where everything means everything and combined, joined and amalgamated we could search the desert terrain and find a solitude and a moment that will be forever etched and our feelings would grow more then we have ever known.

When the sunset and we sat together I never questioned anything. You smiled and the elegance of your womanly figure played out in my dreams for nights on end, all of my senses on fire, hot and bright and burning to be hotter and brighter. Your smile was as eloquent as a diamond and every word you said hung and lingered and fought its way across the distractions of everyday that we didn't see each other. I've never known that feeling of belonging. Like lyrics to a song that fit amazing together with the music and each song we ever heard together has been embedded with your name with your flame that swallows this time and lets me forget and makes me remember that only you can do this to me, only you know how to turn me on and its only you that I'll ever really love………

The entire world rests. No the entire universe caresses the end of my fingertips and my mind is only seeing a reflection of what can potentially be. This whole thing it exists because I am here. I see it, feel it, want it and know only a fraction of what I can be, but each day I learn more and more about who I am. Women wander and scatter through these streets, through to my being and then they drift off on a memory that has no beginning and end. Surely there is a meaning behind every smile, every whisper of the wind and every action I partake in. everything exists because I am here to let it. Purification first starts with a seed of thought. Then it transpires into action, what we believe, what we perceive is boundless and limitless, each day a new moment arises, do we take the plunge or do we remain just existing on the sideline. Maybe everything I have is here because this is what I want. Now what I will have is greater then everything I have ever known. The universe rests on the edges of my fingertips and from this moment on I'll take it all.

It occurred to me. No quicker then it had been thought, that ultimately you were the saving grace that I needed to find. Throughout all the torturous tests that accumulated and built inside me I realised that you were there, somewhere near. I never wanted to fall. I never thought that I was invincible but obviously my only enemy was myself and as giving as I am I'm just as selfish in the way I disregard my knowledge. You're like the candle I need in order to see, if every emotion we feel did indeed have a name then I would be here for eternity trying to explain what it is that I get from you. Why does this interaction between us have to have a name? Why can't it be something that neither of us can decipher? If it is you and it's always been you then I'll find it again. It's not the last time I will feel this way about anyone. What it is, is you've raised the level of what I find amazing. You opened my eyes to beauty I only thought existed elsewhere. You shone rays of perfection and wonderment in corners of my being that were old and forgotten. You made me want to write and be true. My mind has never been so still. Reality has never seemed so easy to control. The road its long and true and as I wandered aimlessly. Hurting myself losing myself, falling I realised now that you saved me. You woke me and I never want to fall again, I don't want to put myself into a compromising position. I am me, and you are you and they are them. And now and forever the stars spell out your name if I squint in the right place. The wind whispers your intentions when its silent the sun shines rays of your beauty. You might be my muse or you might be so much more. I don't know why I feel this way. I don't know if I need to know. Just accept that you shine brighter and sparkle more then any other soul I have encountered. These could be just words or they could be so much more. Will we ever really know?

I know that the universe looms in your eyes and birds sing odes to you and no matter where you are I'm there somewhere like I know you're somewhere there too. Circling, watching, hoping. Knowing. I am the creator of my own destiny and what will be will be. It's young and old and splendid that the road turned and found you. There is solace in silence and I smile because there is so much to smile for. Our souls met sometime. A long time ago. it may have been in ancient Egypt, we may have been lovers or friends. But somewhere our souls intertwined and mingled and knew. There's so much to know. But its in the not knowing that is the most beautiful. It's in the wandering that you acquire feelings and it's in loving that you love. Unconditionally and eternally my world is real and I wouldn't change it or you, not now, not ever.

You were standing there. I could sense there was something unusual about the way you caressed the questions that I wanted to ask. Mesmerised by the equations that blurred and unbalanced the waves of my happiness. The light seeped through the hollow glass, ten thousand fires burnt through my soul and the saxophone played snippets of our jaded hazed fragmented time together. Inhibitions, exhibited on canvas, my thoughts, diamonds in a sea that had no name. Until yesterday I delved into these worries, déjà vu like a song that I knew every word to, backwards and forwards, missing and scattered, temptations had never played out so easily. I was lost somewhere amongst my dignity and a memory that you tried so hard to make me forget. I nurtured the best part of your laughter with my desire and ignorance, I fell into a stupor, your eyes overshadowed the bad and I couldn't help but fall and fall and throughout this feeling that circled like ravens I thought about our future and smiled. Your elegance was always persistent and without you I felt as if I couldn't breathe. I found us scattered on cobbled stoned streets and I'm sorry I lied to you so many time before.........

Your fears meant nothing to me as they appeared and faded long before we had ever met. In September I squandered before my own doubts and came to the conclusion that the only way it was ever going to begin was if I built up enough courage to just tell you that there was something that I couldn't explain, there was a presence that had no words, no amount of poems, stories and ideas could ever explain. I always believe in ideals and notions that are far greater then me. My mind races to you even in the early hours and dreams and all my waking days. Right now as I read this out I never asked for this. Who ever would and all the past events mount up into a circle of what was meant to be. I could understand only a fraction of what you had said. We sat there by the window. I remember glancing over your shoulder and thinking that that moment could have lasted forever. I don't know where to stand. What to think or what to remember to say. Everything feels like it's happened before. Am I stuck in a déjà vu dream or am I vaguely aware that no matter how hard I try I might never be able to escape the reality that it's only you I could ever love?

We were no where, only lying on a soft bed with the red lamp on right next to the draping curtains that we had to move each and every time we wanted to breathe, to open the window that never seemed to open when we tried and the music played and played and we swayed constantly and emotionally and in your ear I whispered wisps of splendour words that only you knew...

Words that we made and the music played and the neighbours swore but before we fell into each other's lives I pictured the soft room it came from another thought that I fought so hard not to remember. I always wanted the best for you I was never the best and the unrest of not knowing whether in the morning you would knock on the door or you would wake up beside me. I never could hold you when we slept, an invasion in my dreams and as placid as you were my breathing hesitated. Then stopped. Then started again. Those abysmal arguments that tore tears in our sheets. The screaming and lovemaking and apologies and lies, it's never going to fade. You're the only woman who could even turn me on with just the look in your eye. We never had to speak and after so many years of words and language to let our souls intermingle in the garden of no language, I languished at the thought and forgot about each and every day that I missed you so much. That room was a world that can never be found again, the crackle of the television and the remote control that found itself so many times in the corridor of another couple's home. Our time together a long, long corridor each door opening into another moment that we can never salvage again. Honey, I called you honey and you were sweet like my childhood dreams. If we met as children we could have built sandcastles all day without a care in the world. Promise me that you'll never forget. Promise me that you'll always remember and I'll hold your name in vain scattered amongst the trees that let me breathe time and time again.

It was never going to be easy. Words left unsaid unplayed and unsung. I drove around aimlessly my mind racing through situations that never existed outside of my mind. The rain pelted down and all this had happened before, not here and not now but somewhere else that I didn't know. I only wanted to be honest. I never asked for the pressure, the outlandish requests that you constantly bombarded me with. If anything gets complicated then you know you have to leave it. But being who we are we tried so hard to control the situation, and my mind repeated words that wouldn't come to my mouth. Between the thinking and saying, the passages were blocked by doubts that had no room to translate or move. Every memory I have ever had is washed away by the insecurities that I keep bringing to the surface. I don't want to say another word. I don't want to pretend to be infatuated by anything that you could ever be. It takes a lot to surprise and overwhelm me. I feel constantly in a state of repetition only because all of this has really happened before, sometime else only slightly different. Time to make new memories, new experiences and new realities. I found you once and sometimes soon I might find you again….

You were constantly illuminated by the anticipation of me wanting you. Like me actual want was a physical presence something like an aura that you could touch. I doubted myself so many times. The voice in my head trying to persuade me that you were right. But I was wrong. As always, my spirit and soul took control. Odes and sonnets were never enough. I was plagued by my past. My words said but also more dramatically I pondered the words I never got the chance to deliver as my doubt washed them out of my mouth. Seagulls stormed the scenery and we sat by oceans as well as forests. If only you had the foresight to see through the façade. Spending time with you I realised confidently that the thought of wanting and needing and missing you was so much greater and forceful then your energy. Maybe I was the only one who didn't drain that away. The one other soul besides yours that could calm oceans of dense hostility. In the scenes of masses of people with eyes and scents and laughter and sex I only wanted to hold you, as I knew that you felt more fragile then you looked. Above the loud music I wanted to whisper to you words that would and could have resonated into your psyche more audible and truer then any lyric to any song written before or since. There are emotions that trickle through this being. But the closest and most innocent I ever was, was when you were close. In some ways not explaining means more. There are so many feelings that have no names yet. So many situations that we have been in that have no definition. If only I could stop labelling and describing everything. Naivety is sacred and when you know nothing else other people fade into water colour backgrounds and I have loved so many times that I have forgotten what it was like to just not love. Every day passed, every word said and song played has evolved me into who I am. Every second that passed until I met you vanished the very moment you parted your lips to say my name. My name, which you say with such perfection. Your eyes that linger in landscapes of a genius' canvas and your soul that evokes millions of desires in me and any other man you pass. I could write for hours and never run out of words. But I'm only interested in the words that haven't been made about you which have never been thought. Because just as sacred as each breath you are the epitome of loveliness and the nexus of every other universe yet to be found.......

Morning light. Dreams parade into other worlds, our sleeps are taunting us constantly with possibilities, tranquil moments that we chase in our waking hours, what are we doing? As the financial world falls to it's knees in front of grandiose demons, we just accept mediocrity like a passing autumn breeze. Have you ever stopped and thought about what it is we are striving for? Weekend shopping is not a luxury it's more like a disease. Indians have the caste system and do you think we do not? Media makes us believe there is a third world, it's us who are slaves to our bills, to debt, to false prophets that dictate what we should drink and consume and why must we pay for their sins? They bombed Iraq but it comes out of our pockets, the banks fall like houses of cards, but it's us who pay the price, why do we need passports to travel the world? It's as much ours as it is theirs, metal detectors and custom officials, its all bullshit. You act in a movie and you earn 40 million dollars a film, you spend your whole life trying to cure Aids or cancer and no body even knows your name, we must stand together, we got to help one another, look in someone's eyes, we are no different, the outer shell is a shell, its what makes us unique, but we have more similarities then differences. Then at 6pm we watch the news and if it's the law of attraction do you think its normal to have forty murder, homicide, crime shows on television every week? We consume ourselves with this shit. Wake up, the world isn't as bad as they make it out to be, go outside. Fear is taught it's not innate we learn to hate, and that seed grows and grows, we all have a purpose we must find it, we can't live our lives for others, you can not look back and think about all the things and words you wanted to say but couldn't, so be you. Be free, let's break the chains of modern day slavery, let's stand as one, the revolution has almost begun, it's not about us versus them, it's about getting back to reality that we are poisoning the planet, when did man first think he owned the world? When did we line up fences and separate land and make it our own? When did we give everything except air a price? We use language to label and dissect, animals look at us with solemn eyes saying 'what the fuck?' we slaughter life to feed our stomachs, we indulge in senseless pleasures like modern day barbarians what will this generation leave as their legacy? Its up to you and me to not get carried away, to understand what is that is, to unlock truths and break down walls, as a child I watched the Berlin wall fall, as a child I watched them sing 'we are the world' as an adolescent I saw what fame did to our idols, drug abused and suicidal, Michael Jackson dancing on top of a limousine outside his court hearing, Rodney King, Tiananmen square, is George Bush any different from any other dictator before? They make the law so how can they break them? The war on terror will go on forever they screen our calls, one global Big brother, lets smile for the satellites, SAT NAV and global roaming, billboards and neon lights, economy and business class, everybody watching the hour glass fade away. They tell us that money makes the world go round its not its greed and it reigns supreme, it sucks you in like a hurricane frenzied snake, buy, buy, bye, your possessions own you instead, you are the aftershave you wear, the colour in your hair, the car that you drive the house where you reside, give me an island in the sun, no television or share market news, no word on the financial blues, so pop up your collar and be free, no one really knows where we want to be, we just need to believe and be true to humanity and our intuition we must feel, and lose our inhibitions and walk through the fire and be true to the one, this life is ours to take, they can try to fence us in but the revolution starts within, seven billion voices can sing, as one. No violence no wars, no guns, if they stopped spending money on weapons they will never need, and look into their souls, and stop the hunger they refuse to feed, they build these weapons to protect themselves from themselves, their only enemies are inner demons, this is the greatest of treasons, to create war without reason, we need to use our powers to help humanity, not bring it to it's knees so please stand up and be seen, its time to raise the screen and turn our reality into our dreams...

If I just told you what I was thinking you wouldn't want to know because you are always scared of the feelings you don't want to remember. In those quiet moments I looked at your side profile and I smiled to myself because seeing you from another angle was always as refreshing as never seeing you before. The contours of your grace. Like crystal glasses that shimmer is a dusty shop that sells glimpses of souls and spirits in tatters. The very second you walked out the door I wished you goodbye so dearly that I felt that if I ever saw you again I might rush to find another breath. You can say almost anything and in that pedicure accent of yours I would believe almost anything and everything that you decided you wanted to believe, I drank wine in a time that I needed to be sober. You never knew what I needed, you only realised right at the end that you had something worthwhile to cherish. Your smile opened up avenues of feelings that had remained hidden for longer then I could comprehend. When the last diamond falls from your eyes and the promise of yesterday's attraction finally fades I'll sit and be drunk on languished memories and smile for you and remember for me...

The lost dedications that fray at the ends. The ends being beginnings and beginnings being moments of solitude all amount to the emptiness that you give and take away without even knowing what you were running from in the first place.I salvaged all I had.You promised me something but remembered not the things that I wanted you too but the moments that I tried hardest to forget.

In the morning I thought about the time that you looked me in the eyes and I knew that day you were only saying it to make me happy. I knew deep down that you never really wanted to say anything. Those hot nights as we drove home, the music we played I told you it was made for you. That we were not alone because all these amazing artists had felt exactly the same way we did all those countless songs with melodies that made my heart bleed and words that I wanted to say to you.

All those versus' chorus' that summed up how I was feeling, each and every moment that we shared. Those car rides, those soft winter mornings, those sticky summer nights when the stars spelt out your name and time rested so far away. The sun rose, oh so quickly and you never had to say a word because we knew each other so well and I could tell you anything and you never judged you could sympathise with my courtesy and I saved you so many times that we just got used to the idea and the notion that we were better then each other.

Now every time I walk past a woman who smells of your perfume, I ponder, and my mind races so fast that if I don't stop and remember that it is not you and it's only some impostor with your sweet scent I might say something to her that only you would know. There are so many reality tattoos that have permanently scared my inner self.

Your favourite food, your favourite novel, all the music, cafes, restaurants, theatres they are all tattoos. Testimonies to our love that crumbled just like your favourite chocolate bar. That is now my favourite chocolate bar that I cant help but notice each and every time I walk anywhere to get away from you. Now this bleeding heart will bleed my dear. And the musicians will write new masterpieces and they will sum up exactly how I'm feeling because I'm never alone in my doubts, I'm never alone in my thoughts.

You're always there permeating the air I breathe, caressing the back of my neck like the wind and taunting my destiny with the possibility that you are somewhere near and I rest assure in the notion that just like that fateful day we met and fell in love and conquered worlds both physical and soulful, that there's always a chance that we could meet again and I'm grateful that we did share those amazing times but above all that I'm just glad that you exist and its you and only you that I can never resist.

Thick smoke drifted through the bar, above the lights like loose clouds floating away from the sunset. It wasn't too dark, seven dying candles lit up the dusty room.

I sat on a round, brown, ashed, bleeding table one of nine tables, reminiscent of little beaten prisoners with no one to love them.

This area was notorious for its small, smoke induced, loin provoked rooms. Speakers playing sad songs sung by hooded voices that crept on you in your sleep, perverting your thoughts and corrupting you to a bottle of wine or two...

If no one was watching I felt like rubbing the inside of my brain with the inside of my palms. Messing my hair up and smoking four cigarettes at once. But I saw her watching. My self conscious self took control and I sat civilized, cauterised, puffing my Marlboro and sipping like a posh fiend on my cabernet sauvignon.

She was older then I. Old enough to have long hair. She hadn't yet reached the age where she could only wear it short. She looked Polish. She looked ravishing. Her eyes bellowed out. Two black olives in a jar of skin. Skin that had once been drained of moisture but put in lazily by a slender hand. Artificial toners and cream that promised to take away wrinkles as well as save the world. Her nose was a small petal, cracked and dry from too much sun. It sat perfectly vertical, like a picket in a fence on a Sunday drive through Pleasantville. Her mouth was perfect for her face. A void of impenetrable loss, forgotten in a vast sea of a one beautiful time. Her lips were two red seals on an iceberg, perfectly rounded. Heaven rested on those lips, taunting my being.

She drank gin I presumed, Gin from a sad glass with sad melting ice. Her long fingers pushed against the glass, holding it up like a man and a lady grasping each others hips on an empty dance floor in the small hours of a melancholy night where the promise of love hides behind the piano player's eyes.

Her body was concealed behind her dress. A navy blue dress that one day she may have worn to a birthday, blue as the blue on a cloudless day melting into tomorrow and an opportunity at finding bliss. Yet in the light of the room it was the blue of a bad dream. One where we are chased and beaten in the end.

I stared at her as she too stared at me. She watched me smoke and drink and her eyes burnt crevices into my eyes, through to my brain, which aroused me to a point I never knew existed until this moment.

I was caught somewhere between my dignity and my untamed beastly animal instinct. I wanted to sleep with her. I wanted to touch every inch of her skin, I wanted to light a thousand candles and dive into pleasures I had read about in novels. If I were a sultan I would make her all 185 women in my harem. I would inspire the gods to fly down to watch and call the dead back by the ferocity of my passion that burned and burned, yearned and yearned to be released.

Her eyes never moved, never flinched. The room swirled as fake as it felt in an old movie set. I saw the air leave her bosom and roll out as smooth as a spring morning. Her body was a canvas and on it I wanted to paint something divine. The music wandered the room like a stranger in a small town. It caressed my ears the way I wanted to caress hers. My glass of wine was almost empty. My cigarette was finished long ago.

Eternity passed in that bar. I was taken to a place whose name I have never found. She watched me stand up. She watched me put my jacket on. She watched me as I paid the cheque and she watched me as I never looked back. I know she did for I saw it a million times after that in my dreams, the anguish in her stare, the desperation of want in her elegance.

I never saw her again.

Epileptic tremors. You flash before my eyes like fragmented holistic fire. You burn the past away like psychotic shards of glass. All that I am, all that I'll ever be, is this right now. My arm savages this pen, like whispers on the tip of your neck in other worlds. I devoured you so many times that our love became an inferno of passion, and in this Worldly ghastly Inferno, the essence of my being was burnt into ash. Ash that rained over every single personified desire that protruded past the hazy glass of your mind. You tore years off the beginning of time. You entrapped me so vividly and ecstatically that I pondered the birth of stars that lived and died. and throughout all of time that ever was and will be, I'll ravish your being with the silhouette of my soul.

We were vying for each other's attention. I watched the trees and they swayed and portrayed beneath the surface was a memory of you. All these pages all these words are they all not the same? But written in another order? Will I ever stop thinking these thoughts? Will I ever find the real thing? See if I do then I might lose the desire for words. I'm at my best when I'm searching to find it, if I don't find it then I suffer for my work, compared to so many people that are lost I should consider myself fortunate that I think and act the way I do, life it's just a carousal sometimes. My body is indeed a temple and I've thrown out all the bad ways that blurred my vision. Feeling the energy and atmosphere I'm clearer headed and poised to accomplish what I need, my only distraction has been myself. I've almost conquered the world outside, my reality is mine, my atmosphere myself, and that's the way it is. Everything just is and it's my time to take it....

Poignant foreshadows of yesterdays desires reflected on the lights. By the window I was in two minds, two worlds. The window was thin, frail, frail like our words that had no echo, frail like the leaves and my outrage, sometimes when we said slanderous things that at the time meant nothing just like now.

I was in two worlds, the world outside, the cold air pushing against the dirty, fragile window, dirty like my thoughts about you, private, bedrooms other universes that we found and never wanted to leave. Hotter then the stars and we saw stars and everything was heightened to points and positions that as teenagers we never dared dream about.

The wet cold dirty air pushing against the window, pushing like the way we pushed together our bodies, speaking in their own dialect, pushing like the way we pushed at our feelings, feeling each others way testing the lengths we could attain in distance to how much we wanted each other and how high we could reach. And me sitting in the transitional position in the café with the warm air, warm like the comforting pleasurable desire that we clung to and our eyes that said novels and each day we were tested, rested and poignant, me in the room that was safe, safe waiting for you, safe as in the way I knew no matter where or why we were together you were always there and when that day came I told you I was ready, ready to take that step, step to you, if I let my mind wander aimlessly through the gardens of yesterday, it revolves around to you.

The air that was warm and easy. Easy like the way in which we could relate and imitate and caress and inspire and everything else faded into oblivion, this café right now, its just a facade you're the only one that needs me and I'm the only one that can open the door to the room you've been searching for, if you make me want to be better then I already am then I'll gladly accept that its you that I should be exclusive with, is it not what we are all aspiring to be, exclusive?

To have an impact on another's world, our world which can not compare, so as I sit in this space by the window, that reflects the two worlds I wait for you, wait as in ponder and anticipate your arrival. Wait as my thoughts carry on past like a train on a track that leads to happiness. I'm clearing out of the fog, the fog being my distractions and vices and as it clears it gets quite obvious that its you that's there and I shouldn't be afraid, I need to take the time for what it is and delve into this and us. My feelings cascading and tearing down walls, walls being my insecurities, but I know you better then you think I do. And as it rains as the sun shines as we embark on this listless wordless boundless journey I take everything you are into my being and every fire that burns inside me burns for you, burns for your eyes and your kiss and as these feelings will never fade and as it rains I sit waiting for you and its everything that I always wanted, you, its you……it's you.

The trepidation of not knowing, reality plays along for the ride amongst the scatter of train rides, conversations, dinners and words that carry more meaning then I ever intended to say or feel. In the emptiness of my bottle of wine I went looking for theories that I wanted to believe, faces that I wanted to love and women that I wanted to spiritually possess. It only matters as much as it ought to; it's only justified when you let your emotions run away and when you forget what you were angry about in the first place. From now on I wont let myself surrender to an unworthy feeling, I will stand disciplined and charged, motivated to make the wrong right again. For too long I surrendered myself to the surface of lesser distracting forces, my reality dictated who I was and I lay there in a comatose state content at the world that wandered aimlessly past my bedroom door without me, its only now that I've woken up, and now I stand healed, ready to dive into the pleasure that eluded me and now that are rightfully mine, that were waiting for me so patiently and that will give me the soul searching rewards that prevailed me for all this time. Opinions of others is only that, our realities co exist but never join, never join and never will...

The chaotic streets, plague my memories, veins as in cobblestones, greyness like the grey in winter twilight. My mind scatters for these memories. This body, this mind, these eyes have seen so much. I have taken in the street poised air of places that I had only dreamt about. The beaches crystallised by the sun that shone in waves of delight. My moments of clarity calmed everything. You were always there. You saw the same things as I, and dreamt the same things as I did.. Yet now I don't feel you. I don't see you and it's hard to not think about it all. My mind is in two, one wants to fight the traps I have set for myself. The other wants to disappear and fade into the night. I hold resentment towards most things. I don't know how to feel for the simple reason that I have never been in this situation. My insecurities will hurt me. My optimism will keep me sane. My laziness I will overcome and my destiny will find me one crisp winter night when I need it to.......

My mind floats and drifts in whispers of nothing. The subtle yet anguished pain in my mind agitates me to sleep in nothing states of nothing. I don't know what time it is, if the sun is out or if the winter days of comfort are over. I don't want to hold onto something that can't be held. Running in circles holding my words as a shield but not knowing if I want to go down or not. Holding the shield to protect myself but always thinking that maybe I'm doing more damage then good. I love her and it feels so right. I have to salvage some sort of will power, some sort of redemption yet nothing seems to be helping, and the words I hold so sacred could come crashing down before my eyes, but time and sorrow are concepts that I want nothing to do with.

I never wanted to be your part time poet, I never wanted more then you could give and it was only the purity of our situation that I felt for so much. It was never going to be easy, while you were looking the other way I would admire you and think to myself that I was lucky that you were so near, I never took it for granted, the late nights, the lack of sleep, the trying to sum up how I felt but what I liked the most was that you often left me speechless, I would hold the pen but nothing would come out, my mind was empty, cleared of the walls and barriers that I had left for myself to overcome, decision after decision, to see you, to let you in, to spend those summer nights holding you while the rest of the world waited, paused. There was no earthquake or problem that could have been that big it would have split us apart. Now I'm left with the memories, this London crisp air refreshes my thoughts, I walk through those cobbled stoned streets but you are not there, I wander around this amazing city, every door a new opening, there is so much to preoccupy my thoughts, but the little things remind me of you and that is one thing I know I can not escape from. I have never plagiarised a feeling, everything I ever felt was raw to the bone. Time away has already taught me many things its taught me to not take the amazing things for granted, and everything is amazing, I want to find traces of the person I was, the one that I lost amongst the situations and environments that sucked the energy out of my marrow, everything is here because I want it to be, it exists because I

am here to see it, feel it and touch it, you are in my memories
and you'll always be there, we never know and not knowing
sometimes is so much better then knowing anything at all.

You are empty, just like your eyes, I bought canvas after canvas, I stopped in dismal shades of regret and the whole time I stood there wondering why I let you in to the inner worlds. You were so up and down you could not even remember which side you should have been on, you lied so many times that you forgot the truth ever existed at all, I know that I need to move on, my priorities are always out of line as I find the next distraction to keep my mind off the issues that I need to address, for so long I didn't care if I woke in the morning, like I was surprised that I came out of it alive, I know that I doubt myself, I let myself fail and I'm scared of the success that I will one day attain. But now the fog has cleared and I'm new and sacred and untied to anything but a feeling of freedom..

Enraptured novice. You hesitate upon the scent of my being. You cause order in chaos if you can define order as a sentimental feeling of longing that glosses over my soul. In the shadow of night, like starving serpents I wait silently in the wallowing hours between the moments we touch, a thousand memories are born and lost all in the same second of every moment, and in the minutes that we spend together I ponder every star that ever shone on this earth. Time evaporates into slithers of nothing. And as timeless and radiant as a diamond you enlighten the universe with just the glimmer in your eyes.

City rooftops beckon like children in Easter, the cool winter night, the air hits my face and the further from grace I go the longer and softer it will be to find what I have lost. My body shows me new pains, scars from hedonistic ways. I walk the alley ways and take in the moment it all rests its head on the pillow of yesterday, all I have ever had are these thoughts and my feelings that drive through states to find peace, if I ever said or did anything that wasn't me then I tasted the etches and outlines of my mistakes, but my mind overcomes the bitterness and I file though the night and I see faces and eyes that are not mine but only mirrors of other people and lives that I could have been but am not, and the Hare Krishna's chant and dance, worldly possessions erased and I stroll now with my collar up thinking about all the possessions that own me instead, I crumble at the sound of your voice. I chase rainbows and fragments of what could have been, its all ok now, transporting in luminous states of not understanding I travelled along roads that I didn't belong on, I caressed the cheeks of girls that I should have known better then to get mixed up with, being in the invincible state I spoke on rooftops about notions and ideals that I wanted to live by but forgot about the second I opened the door to step outside. The world frightened me and hurt me until the day I realised that it was myself that hurt myself. My choices gone, the past erased, what matters is right now and right now there is only me and I can't escape from myself anymore. I cant run from who I am like I tried to for so long, so now I'll stand alone and listen to my own voice and heart and soul its here because I am here it exists because I'm here to make it exist, so now I am awake and now I'm stronger and I can only make it right again, like I know I will, I flash past gleaming lights and smiles, I am me and that what I'm always going to be just me and I would never want to ask for anything more.

The day fills itself with questions and resolutions, I never wanted to be any more then a glimmer in your imagination, my silent fingers passed through your quiet hair, the bottles of yesterday washed themselves in the morning, in the passing of a thought a memory you came and moved so silently that if I insinuated anything more than an honest proposal of intimacy I apologise profusely. In connecting the moments that make the days healthy, I outweighed the presence of guys that didn't understand not a word that you whispered that night under the shelter of the bus stop where I almost proposed my eternal love for you. If you ever felt anything that wasn't an honest feeling tell me now before this moment passes and as it moves right now we will never have it again, it washes up somewhere else, just like all those countless words that I almost said that came to my mind but vanished at the end of my crazy feelings that ran faster then my spirit and nearly suffocated this world, if I only breathed for you, every second was worth it, without question or doubt they were islands of hope in waters of my infatuation. I rest for today, but as we both don't know tomorrow and as my lips crave yours I'll find the solitude that what I create today in my mind tomorrow I might find you and me dancing to the guitar that slept in the corner of yesterday's dream and nothing will be ours and the world will sparkle silently and forever.

Fragments of wasted desire. Wash up along the shores of other peoples dreams. Poignant feelings that rise up from the flames of the wrong. I played amongst the shadows. Afraid to see a reflection of what it was I was doing

And through the loose translation of rising ghosts. I heard sounds and words that haunted my dreams. My dreams took me to times of the past. To secret rooms with secret people, who did everything in their power to hide the truth before my eyes. And there I was crying for peace. Peace of mind and waves of sanity. My heart bleeding for souls lost, all because they worshipped the same God but with a different name. This world is broken down into light and dark. Shadow and night and through the mind and eyes of other spirits I was taught what was right and what was wrong. In each of us the truth is concealed. This world is only a reflection of a dream. We are all part of something dreamer. Something that is only tangible when peace is found. In the next year the world will realize the lies and the truth will rain down on us like emasculated shapes of love.

My eyes. They visit worlds when I sleep. These waking hours, a reflection on a faded glance of something else. I chase you throughout all the haze. Like crystal embers that burn eternally. You know my mind even before my mind knows myself. You are the words in between the spaces, beyond the faces that watch from a distance. I caress the base of your neck. The heavenly spot where your womanly divine essence permeates into my soul. Drawn between the sheets like immaculate sculptors of other worldly Gods. In all that I am, in all that I'll ever be, without you nothing seems to exist. As pure as the Suns rays on the side of this earth with just the glimmer in your eye, right before you blink, you astound me. In that very moment you radiate something that has yet to be defined with every pore of my yearning skin I salvage your energy, I let it wash over this grey world to make me see colour once more. Exquisite to touch, your lips burn rings into my being. Reminding me constantly that in every angle of perfection the world spins and spins until all of us are dizzy with lust.

©Nihal Bhagwandas 2013.